Who Pooped in the Black Hills?

Written by Gary D. Robson

Illustrated by Robert Rath

FARCOUNTRY
PRESS

HELENA, MONTANA

To the rangers and park staff
who help me so much with my books.
– Gary

For Lucy and Thomas, my poop experts.
– Robert

ISBN 10: 1-56037-387-3
ISBN 13: 978-1-56037-387-2

For more information on our books,
write Farcountry Press, P.O. Box 5630, Helena, MT 59604;
call (800) 821-3874; or visit www.farcountrypress.com.

Library of Congress Cataloging-in-Publication Data

Robson, Gary D.
  Who pooped in the Black Hills? / written by Gary D. Robson ; illustrated by Robert Rath.
     p. cm.
  ISBN 13: 978-1-56037-387-2
  ISBN 10: 1-56037-387-3
  1. Animal tracks--Black Hills (S.D. and Wyo.)--Juvenile literature. I. Rath, Robert, ill. II. Title.
QL768.R59 2006
599.09783'9--dc22

2006014536

Created, produced, and designed in the United States.
Manufactured by
Everbest Printing
334 Huanshi Road South
Dachong Western Industrial District
Panyu, Guangdong, China
in April 2013
Printed in China.

17 16 15 14 13   4 5 6 7 8

"Are we there yet?" Michael said as he squirmed in the back seat. "We've been driving forever."

"We're almost there!" said Dad.

Mom pointed out the window and said, "Look! There's Mount Rushmore. Our first stop in the Black Hills."

3

The kids had snacks, iPods, and their favorite books, but they were tired of riding in the car!

"When we get to Mount Rushmore," said Mom, "we'll go for a walk."

"Michael's too scared to walk in the woods," said Michael's older sister, Emily. "He's afraid he'll get eaten by a mountain lion." She growled and made her fingers look like claws.

"Stop it, Emily," said Mom. "Nobody's getting eaten by anything."

Michael was excited about the trip, but Emily was right. He *was* nervous.

He was reading a wildlife book and the mountain lions were really scary!

the STRAIGHT **POOP**

Never hike by yourself. Mountain lions almost never bother people hiking in groups.

"I *am* kind of scared of mountain lions," Michael admitted.

"Don't worry," Dad told him. "Mountain lions are scared of people, too. We probably won't even see one."

"We'll learn all about mountain lions without ever getting close to one," Mom added.

After a bathroom break, the kids were ready to explore.

"Let's climb the rocks!" Michael said.

"We have to stay on the trails here at Mount Rushmore," Mom said. "We're not allowed to go into the woods."

the STRAIGHT POOP

The faces of American presidents George Washington, Thomas Jefferson, Theodore Roosevelt, and Abraham Lincoln are carved into the rock at Mount Rushmore National Monument.

the STRAIGHT **POOP**

Porcupines love to eat bark. Sometimes they climb trees and eat the bark all the way around, killing the trees.

Dad smiled. "By the word 'sign,' I mean a clue that an animal has left behind," he explained.

"Like this," Mom said. "See where the bark has been chewed off of those trees? That's a sign of a porcupine having its lunch."

Michael forgot all about mountain lions and was excited to search for clues. "Look! Footprints!" he said.

"That's right," said Mom. "Those are porcupine tracks. You can see where it dragged its tail in the middle."

the STRAIGHT POOP

It's best to leave porcupines alone. Their quills are very sharp, and even though they can't throw them at you, they can still stick you if you get too close.

Mom pointed to something next to the tracks. It was lumpy, bumpy, and brown.

"This is porcupine scat," Mom said.

"*Scat*?" asked Emily. "What's *scat*?"

"It's a word hikers and trackers use for animal poop," Dad replied.

The STRAIGHT POOP

The pasqueflower is South Dakota's state flower. It blooms in spring.

"See, Michael," said Dad. "We don't have to get up close to an animal to learn about it. Instead of a close encounter of the *scary* kind, we'll have a close encounter of the *poopy* kind."

Everybody laughed, and Mom made a gross-out face.

13

At their next stop in the Black Hills, the kids were eager to look for clues.

"I found more scat," said Michael, trying to sound grown up. "It looks like what we clean out of my bunny's cage at home."

"It looks a little like rabbit scat," said Dad. "But it's from a deer."

"How can you tell?" Emily asked.

"Rabbit scat is small and round, like little balls," Mom explained. "Deer scat is shaped more like jellybeans."

Emily laughed when she thought of poop shaped like jellybeans.

DEER SCAT

JACKRABBIT SCAT

JELLYBEANS

the STRAIGHT POOP

Rabbits eat their own scat! They do this to get as much nutrition from the food as they can. The little brown balls are scat that's already been through the rabbit twice.

15

Michael spotted something on the ground.
He got scared when he saw it was a deer antler.

"Oh, no!" he said. "Did a mountain lion eat the deer?"

"The deer is safe," Dad said. "Every year, their antlers
fall off, and then they grow bigger ones."

the STRAIGHT POOP

Do you know the difference between a horn and an antler? Deer have antlers, and bighorn sheep have horns. Antlers are shaped like branches and fall off every year. Horns never fall off and keep growing for the animal's entire life.

"Are those deer tracks over there?" asked Michael.

"Good eye!" said Mom. "See how the tracks are split down the middle? Deer hooves have two parts."

"What are these little marks?" asked Emily, pointing to two funny little dents behind each track.

the STRAIGHT POOP

Dewclaws don't always show in deer tracks. They sometimes can be seen when the deer leaves tracks in mud or snow.

DEWCLAW

"Those are from the deer's *dewclaws*," explained Mom.

Emily thought Mom was trying to fool her. "Deer don't have claws!" she said.

"Dewclaws are small claws on an animal's legs," Mom explained. "Lots of animals have them, including dogs and cats. Even animals with hooves, like deer."

"This deer was in a hurry," said Mom, as she studied the ground.

Michael and Emily went over to look.

"How can you tell?" asked Emily. She was having fun figuring out the clues and hadn't teased her brother all afternoon.

"The hoofprints get very far apart here," Mom explained. "And the front prints are behind the back prints."

"The deer was walking backwards?" said Emily.

"No, it was galloping. Something scared it and it was moving fast," Mom said.

GALLOPING

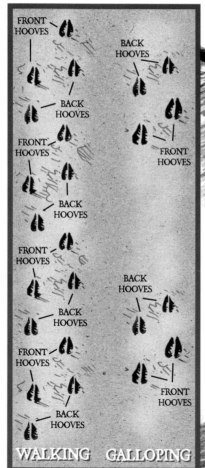

FRONT HOOVES

BACK HOOVES

BACK HOOVES

FRONT HOOVES

FRONT HOOVES

FRONT HOOVES

BACK HOOVES

FRONT HOOVES

BACK HOOVES

BACK HOOVES

FRONT HOOVES

BACK HOOVES

FRONT HOOVES

BACK HOOVES

WALKING   GALLOPING

the STRAIGHT POOP

Animals' back legs are also called "hind" legs.

20

"Here's what scared the deer," said Dad. "There are coyote tracks all around here."

The family rushed over to look.

"They look like dog tracks," said Michael.

"That's because coyotes are members of the dog family," said Dad.

Mom added, "Their scat looks like dog poop, too, except that coyote scat has bits of bones and hair in it from the animals they eat."

"Yuck!" said Emily.

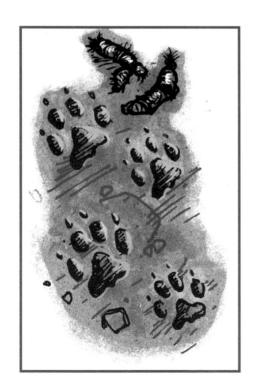

the STRAIGHT POOP

Scientists study what coyotes eat by examining coyote scat.

"Some of these coyote tracks are very small," said Mom, "like they're from pups. I'll bet there's a den nearby. We should leave so we don't disturb them."

"Let's drive out onto the plains now and see what else we can find," said Dad.

the STRAIGHT POOP

Coyotes will eat just about anything they can catch, and they'll steal leftovers from other predators, too.

23

Emily stared out the window. She imagined all the animals on the plains, stomping around on the dirt making footprints, and pooping on the ground, leaving behind scat.

Suddenly a herd of animals appeared.

Emily thought they looked like horses, but different.

Mom said, "Those are burros."

Michael squealed when he looked out the window and saw the car surrounded by burros. "They're attacking us!" he cried.

"It's okay," said Dad. "They're just looking for food. We're not going to feed them, though. They may look tame, but they are still wild animals."

the STRAIGHT POOP

Burros and horses are different. Burros have light-colored noses, dark crosses on their backs and shoulders, and dark outlines around their ears.

Michael was relieved when they escaped
the burros and Dad parked the car.

"Do you notice anything funny about
the ground here, kids?" Dad asked.

"The ground's all full of holes," said Michael.

"And there's a bunch of scat, but it looks different," said Emily.

"This is a prairie dog town," said Mom. "Prairie dogs are rodents, related to mice and hamsters."

"They like to live in big groups," Dad added. "There can be thousands of them in one small town, and there used to be big prairie dog towns with millions of them."

"And there are some big animals that like to share land with prairie dogs, too," said Mom.

BISON
FROM AMERICA

WATER BUFFALO
FROM INDIA

CAPE BUFFALO
FROM AFRICA

"Bison?" said Emily. "I thought Mom said these were buffalo tracks."

"They're really called bison," Dad explained. "Early settlers called them buffalo because they look like buffalo from other parts of the world. The name stuck, and lots of people still call them buffalo."

"These smaller tracks must be from baby bison," said Michael.

"No," said Emily. "Look how pointy they are. I think they're deer tracks."

"You both have good ideas," said Mom, "but these are pronghorn tracks. You can tell because the outer part of the hoof curves in. A deer print curves out."

BISON
TRACK

PRONGHORN
TRACKS

"Pronghorns and bison sometimes hang out together," said Dad, "and both of them like prairie dog towns."

The STRAIGHT POOP

The pronghorn's scientific name means "antelope goat," but it isn't really related to an antelope or a goat.

the STRAIGHT POOP

Pronghorns are some of the fastest animals in the world. They can run more than 60 miles per hour—about as fast as a car on a highway!

As the family moved back into the trees, Emily spotted something new.

"What are *these* tracks?" she asked. "They're really funny-looking."

"Those are wild turkey tracks," Dad replied.

the STRAIGHT POOP

Benjamin Franklin wanted the wild turkey to be America's national bird, instead of the bald eagle.

"Is this mountain lion scat?" asked Michael.

"It sure is," said Dad. "The mountain lion tried to bury it, but the ground is too hard right here."

"The scat has hair and bits of bone in it, just like the coyote scat did," Michael pointed out. "That means that they eat other animals."

the STRAIGHT POOP

Mountain lions may be the biggest cat in America, but they still bury their scat just like a housecat.

Emily laid her hand next to the track. "It's awfully big," she said.

"That's right," Mom said. "A mountain lion weighs as much as I do, and a big one can weigh more than Dad!"

As the family ate dinner that night, everyone talked about how much fun they had.

"We didn't see very many animals," said Emily, "but it seemed like we did!"

44

Everyone laughed when Michael said, "And I didn't get scared once!"

COYOTE

 FRONT

BACK

Four toes on each foot. Claw marks usually can be seen.

Scat is very dark in color, narrow on the ends, and usually contains hair.

MOUNTAIN LION

LEADING TOE · LEFT FRONT

DENT

RIGHT BACK

Four toes on each foot. Tracks are bigger than a coyote's, but claws don't show.

Scat is rarely seen because they bury it.

EASTERN COTTONTAIL RABBIT

FRONT

BACK

Four toes on each foot. Small tracks are mostly filled in between toes because of furry feet. Claw marks sometimes show.

Scat is small, brown balls.

PORCUPINE

FRONT

BACK

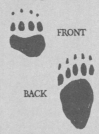

Four toes on front feet. Five toes on back feet. Tail drag marks sometimes show.

Scat pellets are larger than deer scat.

PRAIRIE DOG

FRONT

BACK

Four toes on the front feet, with long claws. Five toes on the back feet. Slender toes connect to back "pad."

Scat is bigger than deer scat. Pellets are often connected by fibers.

SCAT NOTES

MULE DEER	PRONGHORN	BURRO	BISON	WILD TURKEY

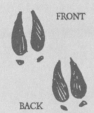
FRONT
BACK

FRONT
BACK

FRONT
BACK

FRONT
BACK

MULE DEER

Tracks are pointy and split into two parts. The sides of the tracks curve out.

Scat is oval-shaped like jellybeans.

PRONGHORN

Tracks are pointy and split into two parts like deer tracks, but they curve in on the sides, and have "bulbs" in back.

Scat pellets are similar to deer's, but they tend to stick together more.

BURRO

Tracks have one part, not two. They are larger than deer or pronghorn tracks.

Scat is in chunks, with pieces of grass often visible.

BISON

Tracks are split into two parts but are much larger than deer or pronghorn tracks and are blunt on the tips.

Scat is similar to "cow patties."

WILD TURKEY

Three slender toes point forward, and one toe points backward. Sometimes the back toe doesn't show.

Scat is long and narrow. Fresh scat is brown in the middle and greenish-white on the ends.

ABOUT the AUTHOR and ILLUSTRATOR

GARY ROBSON lives in Montana near Yellowstone National Park, where he and his wife own a bookstore and tea bar. Gary has written dozens of books and hundreds of articles, mostly related to science, nature, and technology.
www.robson.org/gary

ROBERT RATH is a book designer and illustrator living in Bozeman, Montana. Although he has worked with Scholastic Books, Lucasfilm, and Montana State University, his favorite project is keeping up with his family.

BOOKS IN THE WHO POOPED IN THE PARK?™ SERIES:

Acadia National Park
Big Bend National Park
Black Hills
Cascades
Colorado Plateau
Death Valley National Park
Glacier National Park
Grand Canyon National Park
Grand Teton National Park
Great Smoky Mountains National Park
Northwoods
Olympic National Park
Red Rock Canyon National Conservation Area
Rocky Mountain National Park
Sequoia and Kings Canyon National Parks
Shenandoah National Park
Sonoran Desert
Yellowstone National Park
Yosemite National Park